# Riding High

JANET DAILEY

SIGNAL HILL

This book is fiction. The author invented the names, people, places, and events. If any of them are like real places, events, or people (living or dead), it is by chance.

SIGNAL HILL®

Copyright © 1994 by Janet Dailey
Signal Hill Publications
A publishing imprint of Laubach Literacy International
1320 Jamesville Avenue
Syracuse, NY 13210-0131

Printed in the United States of America

Illustration by Cheri Bladholm
Original cover art by Ron Hall

9 8 7 6 5 4 3 2 1

Library of Congress Cataloging-in-Publication Data

Dailey, Janet.

Riding high / Janet Dailey.

p. cm. — (Janet Dailey's love scenes)

ISBN 1-56420-098-1
1. Motion picture actors and actresses—Colorado—
Fiction. 2. Man-woman relationships—Colorado—
Fiction. I. Title II. Series: Dailey, Janet. Janet
Dailey's love scenes.

PS3554.A29R55    1994
813'.54—dc20                          94-18547
                                      CIP

# Chapter 1

"I won't do it! No way! Forget it!" Deke Flanders leaned back in his chair and propped his cowboy boots on the top of his desk. A deep frown creased his handsome face as he spoke into the phone.

"Oh, come on, Deke," said the voice on the other end of the line. "Do it for old times' sake. We've been friends for years. I'd do anything for *you*."

"But *I* wouldn't ask you to teach a bratty movie star how to ride a horse—in *one* weekend." Deke pushed back his Stetson with his thumb.

"But Victoria is beautiful," Martin argued. "Do you know how many men would kill for this chance?"

"Kill, huh? Well, Victoria and I might wind up murdering each other. Have you thought about that?"

"No, you won't. I promise. You're wrong about Victoria. She can be really nice." Martin paused, then added, "When she wants to be."

"Sure," Deke sighed. This battle of wills had been going on for half an hour, and he was getting tired. "I've read the papers," he said. "She's spoiled rotten."

"She's the star of my next movie," Martin replied. "We start filming on Monday. She has to be able to ride a horse by then."

Deke knew he was about to give in. He couldn't help himself. Martin Conroy was the director who had helped him get into the movies years ago.

Deke had made a good living as a stunt cowboy. He rode wild horses and roped getaway steers on the screen. And sometimes he broke bottles and chairs over the bad guys' heads in a saloon. Deke loved his job and his ranch in Colorado. And he owed it all to Martin.

"Has she ever been on a horse before?" Deke asked, sounding defeated.

"She says she has," Martin replied. "But you wouldn't know it by watching her ride."

"Oh, wonderful. I can see I have my work cut out for me."

"Great!" Martin said. Deke hated how happy he sounded. Martin had won—again. "She'll be at your ranch first thing Friday morning."

"Oh, goody," Deke said as he hung up the phone. "I can hardly wait."

He rose from his chair and stretched his long, lanky body. A magazine lay on his desk. He picked it up and flipped to the picture he had seen that morning. Victoria Thornton stood in front of her Hollywood mansion, wearing an elegant evening gown. She was about to step into a red Ferrari that must have cost as much as Deke's ranch house.

The woman's pale green eyes seemed to stare into his. Their intensity went through him like liquid fire. She was a strong-minded woman, that was for sure. Teaching her anything would be a challenge.

But Martin was right: She *was* beautiful.

# Chapter 2

"No, Martin. I'm not going to do it, and you can't make me." Victoria Thornton stood in the middle of the studio stage, facing Martin. Around them was a country kitchen set, where some of the scenes from the new movie would be shot.

But Victoria wasn't aware of her surroundings. She was so angry that all she could see was red. Her arms were crossed over her chest, and she wore a glare on her pretty face.

Martin walked closer to her and patted her shoulder. "Deke is a great guy. Really. He'll make it easy for you. You'll see."

"No! I don't know why you keep pushing this horse thing." Victoria tossed her long red curls behind her shoulder and walked around the fake wall.

She picked up her leather coat from a stack of plywood props. "I told you, I *hate* horses," she said. "They smell bad. They're big and they step on your feet. If you don't give them carrots or apples, they bite you. They have flies, Martin. I hate flies, too."

Martin caught up with her. Gently he took her arm and guided her toward the door. "Now, now. Deke knows how important you are to me. He won't let anything bad happen to you. That's a promise."

Victoria knew he was flattering her to get on her good side. She was only important to Martin because of all the millions he had invested in this movie.

"Please," he said. "If you do this, I'll owe you one."

She thought for a minute. It was always a good idea to have the director owe you at the beginning of a movie. You never knew when you might need to cash in the favor.

"You'll owe me a *big* one," she said, giving in.

He grabbed her and planted a big kiss on her cheek.

"You're a doll!" he said.

"Yeah, yeah. No problem. Anything for you, Martin."

Victoria slipped on her jacket and headed out the door. Once outside the building, she leaned against the wall to catch her breath. Her throat felt like it was about to close and choke her. She could feel her heart pounding.

Was she really going to do this? A sick feeling crept over her at the thought. Some people were afraid of spiders. Some were scared of snakes. But she would rather handle a black widow or play with an angry rattler than get on a horse.

*You're being dumb, Vickie,* she told herself. *It's just a horse.*

*Sure, a great big horse with biting teeth and kicking hooves and . . . I can't do it,* she thought, panic rising. *I can't.*

But she knew she had to do it. Once and for all, she had to face this silly fear and put it behind her.

Just thinking about Friday morning made her pulse race. She had to get this fear under control before she arrived at that ranch in Colorado. If she didn't, the horse wouldn't need to stomp her flat or eat her alive. She would just die of heart failure the moment she saw it.

# Chapter 3

Deke leaned one arm on top of the pitchfork and wiped the sweat off his brow with the back of his hand. A lock of dark hair hung over his dirt-smeared forehead. He looked at his watch. Ten-thirty. She would be arriving soon.

Glancing down at the muck on his jeans, he thought he should go into the house and change clothes. Then he decided not to. If Miss Victoria wanted to know what it was like to be a cowboy, she might as well see the whole show.

A cloud of dust coming down the road told him that his student had arrived. At least she was on time. But what was that she was riding in?

As the car drew nearer, he realized it was a white limousine. A *huge* white limousine. While on rodeo tours he had lived in trailers smaller than that. He grinned when he saw how much dust was collecting on the white finish.

"Might as well get used to eating a little dirt, lady," he said under his breath.

The car pulled to a stop in front of the house. He propped the pitchfork against the side of the barn and strolled across the field to meet his new student.

A driver stepped out of the car, wearing a formal black suit. He opened the door and Deke saw a long pair of blue-jeaned legs slide out. The legs were followed by the rest of the most beautiful woman he had ever seen.

She was dressed in western garb: a plaid shirt, jeans, and boots. The clothes were new, Deke noticed. He didn't know whether to laugh or to be touched that she had bought this costume for the weekend. The boots were going to kill her feet. And the inside seam of the jeans would rub her thighs raw when she rode.

*Oh, well,* he thought. *What else can you expect from a city slicker?*

He ran his fingers through his hair and wished he had changed clothes. After all, it wasn't every day a movie star came to the ranch.

"Hello," he called out. "Welcome to Flanders' Folly."

"Thanks," she said, choking on the dust that swirled around her.

He couldn't help noticing how her red hair shone in the morning sun, like a polished copper kettle. He wished she would take off her sunglasses so he could see her eyes.

She moved gracefully toward him and held out her hand.

"You must be Deke," she said. "I'm Victoria Thornton."

"I know," he said, feeling as awkward as a high school kid. He took her hand in his and was surprised at the firmness of her handshake. "I'm a fan of yours."

She took off her sunglasses and fixed him with the same intense green stare that he had seen in the magazine.

"Really?" she asked.

He laughed softly. "Well, I am now."

"That's good," she said. "It'll help us get through the weekend more easily. I have to tell you, I'm not looking forward to this."

Her bluntness put Deke off a bit. He hadn't been looking forward to it either. But he was well-mannered enough not to say so the moment they met. His smile faded and he crossed his arms over his chest.

The driver went to the back of the car and pulled four large suitcases from the trunk.

"If you'll just show Dennis where to put those—" she said.

Something about the airy wave of her hand annoyed Deke.

"Just drop them there where you stand, Denny," he replied.

Victoria looked down at the dusty dirt road and at her luggage. "Excuse me, Mr. Flanders. But those bags are Louis Vuittons."

He recognized the luggage's expensive brand name, but couldn't resist teasing her.

"Well, I reckon Mr. Vuitton is going to be pretty upset when he realizes you've got his suitcases." He turned his back to her and began walking toward the house. "The airlines get my luggage mixed up sometimes, too."

It really was against his Southern upbringing to walk in front of a lady. But he couldn't help feeling a little pleased with himself for putting Miss Priss in her place. If she knew who was boss from the start, this whole ordeal would go more smoothly.

He led them into the ranch house. Victoria was pouting. Dennis struggled with the bags. Taking pity on him, Deke grabbed two of them.

"This way," he said. He headed through the living room toward the hall.

He braced himself for a sarcastic comment from the movie star about his house. But she smiled as she looked around at the stone fireplace, the redwood walls, and the rustic furniture.

"Very nice," she said. "Feels homey."

"I like it." Deke nodded toward the hall. "Your room is this way."

"I get to sleep in the house?" She tossed her red hair back over her shoulder. "I thought you'd stick me out in the barn."

"I wanted to, but Maggie didn't approve."

"Who's Maggie?" she asked.

"You'll meet her later."

He took her to the small bedroom at the end of the hall. "I washed the sheets," he said, pointing to the iron bed with its colorful red-and-blue quilt. He nodded toward the guest bathroom across the hall. "And I put out soap and towels and stuff in there."

"Gee, just like the Plaza," she said, running her finger through the dust on the dresser.

"I don't dust," he said. "There's no point. A week later, you just have to do it again."

Victoria walked over to the window and looked outside. "No point in washing windows, either, I see," she said. "Come spring, they'd just be dirty again."

"You got it."

Deke tossed the two suitcases on top of the bed and motioned for Dennis to do the same. The driver placed his two carefully beside the dresser.

"Will that be all, ma'am?" Dennis asked.

"Yes, I suppose so." She gave Deke a look that made him wish he could apply his boot to her shapely fanny.

"Then I'll return on Sunday night," Dennis said as he tipped his hat to her.

"Don't be late," she called after him. "I have a feeling I'm going to be eager to leave."

Deke left her in the bedroom and hurried after the driver. "Yeah, Dennis," he called across the yard as the man got into the limo to leave. "Don't be late. In fact, why don't you come back early. *Very* early. Say, in about ten minutes."

# Chapter 4

"Lesson one—make friends with your horse," Deke said. He led Victoria into the stable and toward a canvas bag in the corner. He reached into the bag and pulled out a couple of carrots.

"I've never had a horse for a friend," Victoria said. Her hands shook as she took one of the carrots from him.

"Then you don't know what you've missed," he replied. "A horse is a man's best friend."

"I thought that was a dog."

Deke laughed. "Boy, you *do* need lessons."

He walked through the stable and out the other side. She followed, her heart pounding. She could feel the sweat breaking out on her forehead.

Two horses were in the corral. A spirited black gelding paced from one end of the pen to the other. An old brown mare stood quietly at the fence, reaching to nibble grass on the other side.

"This is Black Fury," Deke said as he walked toward the gelding. "He's yours for the day. Better make friends."

"Black Fury!" Victoria almost screamed the words. "You expect me to get on a horse named Black Fury? You must be crazy!"

"That's right. He's the best choice for you. Really." Deke laughed, and Victoria felt her anger rising, along with her fear. He seemed to be enjoying this.

She looked at Black Fury, who snorted and shook his head. His muscles rippled beneath his sleek hide. He was huge. He looked at least nine feet tall to Victoria. Maybe twelve. She would have to use a ladder just to mount him.

No. She couldn't do it. She just couldn't.

"I'm not going to get on that animal, Mr. Flanders," she said firmly. "Don't you have something that's a little more . . . more tame?"

She spotted the old mare at the fence and pointed at her. "Like that one?"

"Who? Old Maggie?" He shook his head. "Believe me, you don't want to ride her."

Victoria watched the old horse as she moved along the fence, her head down, her steps slow.

"She's *exactly* what I want," Victoria argued as she walked toward the mare. "Here, horsey, horsey. Nice horsey," she said, holding out her carrot.

"Hey, don't do that!" Deke ran to her and grabbed her hand.

"Don't do what?" she asked.

"Don't hold the carrot out like that. You'll get your fingers bitten off."

Her fingers bitten off! That was exactly what had happened in her latest nightmare.

"Horses don't see very well," Deke said. "And especially old Maggie. They can't tell the difference between a carrot and a finger."

He placed the carrot in the palm of her hand and wrapped her fingers around it. "When you offer it to a horse, hold it so that it's sticking out of your fist. Like this."

Although Victoria was angry at him and scared silly, she was aware of his warm hand around hers. Most of the men she knew had soft hands. His were rough, and she found she liked the way they felt against hers.

For a moment she looked up into his eyes. Something in the way he was looking at her said that he was aware of her, too.

"You really will do much better with Black Fury," he said. "Trust me."

Trust him? She didn't trust *anyone* enough to get within six feet of that prancing, snorting bundle of rippling muscles.

She pulled her hand away from his and turned her back to him. "Here, Maggie," she said, holding out the carrot to the mare. "Come get the nice carrot, Maggie."

Maggie perked up right away. Her ears twitched, and she began to walk toward Victoria.

"Oh, no," Victoria whispered. She had to fight the urge to run—or scream—or cry—or all three. The horse was coming right to her.

Her hand began to shake so badly that she nearly dropped the carrot.

*Stop it!* she told herself. *It's just a tired old horse. It probably doesn't have the energy to even . . .*

The horse peeled back its lips and the big, yellow teeth opened.

Victoria closed her eyes and steeled herself for the worst. A second later, the carrot was gone.

She opened her eyes and looked at her empty hand. Four fingers and a thumb.

"See. That wasn't so bad," she heard Deke say. "Now you've got a friend for life."

"Does that mean she won't bite me, step on me, or throw me off?"

"Well . . . I wouldn't go that far," he drawled. "Maggie may be old, but she still has a few tricks up her sleeve. Wait until you try to bridle her."

"Me? *I* have to do it?"

"Of course. Martin told me to give you the full course."

"I'll have to thank him the next time I see him," she said through gritted teeth.

# Chapter 5

Deke took two bridles from hooks on the stable wall and tossed one to Victoria. He walked over to Black Fury. The big horse stood, as gentle as a puppy, as Deke put the bridle on him. He explained the steps to her. It seemed simple enough. She began to cheer up a bit. Maybe this wouldn't be so hard after all.

But when she walked toward Maggie, the old horse suddenly came alive. Her ears pricked up. She snorted and took off across the corral.

"Oh, yeah," Deke said with a grin. "I forgot to tell you, Maggie's lazy. She'll do anything to get out of being ridden."

Victoria watched as her mount scampered around the pen. Maggie's tail was high in the air. She seemed to be enjoying herself, playing games with this silly woman who was trying to catch her.

Deke leaned against the fence with one leg propped up. He was chewing on a piece of straw. He, too, seemed to enjoy watching Victoria run around until her tongue was almost hanging out.

After ten minutes of the chase, Victoria stopped in the middle of the corral, panting. Sweat was rolling down her face.

"Well, Mr. Flanders," she said, trying to catch her breath. "Do you have any words of wisdom? Now would be a great time to offer them."

"Nope. You're doing fine, Miss Thornton," he said. "Just keep at it. She'll get tired pretty soon."

Victoria looked at the horse, who seemed more frisky than ever.

"Gee, thanks," she said, giving him a dirty look. "What a great teacher you are!"

He shrugged his broad shoulders and laughed at her. Victoria's temper rose. She didn't care if he was handsome and looked wonderful in his tight jeans. He was a creep. And she had had enough of this darned horse, too.

After chasing Maggie a few more minutes, Victoria realized she would never catch her this way. The horse had four legs. She had only two. This wasn't going to work.

*Better try something else*, she told herself.

The horse might be faster, but she was smarter. At least she hoped she was.

She had won an Oscar for her acting. Maybe now was a good time to use her acting talents.

Slowly she walked to the center of the corral and sat down in the dirt. From the corner of her eye she could see Deke watching her closely.

She drew her knees up and rested her forearms across them. Then she buried her face in her arms and began to make soft crying sounds. She thought she heard footsteps—*boot* steps—walking in her direction. Peeking, she saw Deke coming toward her.

"Stop," she hissed. "Go away."

He gave her a puzzled look, then went back to his place at the fence.

She began the crying sounds again, louder than before. She peered through the curtain of her red hair and watched Maggie. The mare stopped trotting around and stood still, looking at her. Victoria could see that she was wary of coming closer.

*Smart horse,* she thought. *But she's female, and that means she's curious.*

Victoria continued crying. Sure enough, the mare began to walk toward her. It was working. She came closer and closer. Finally, Victoria could feel a velvety nose nuzzling her neck and cheek.

Slowly she reached up and stroked the soft nose. "That's a girl," she crooned. "That's my pretty girl. What a beautiful horse you are."

Rising, she gently slipped the bit into Maggie's mouth. She drew the leather straps up and over her ears as Deke had shown her. The whole time she talked in a soft, soothing voice. Finally, she fastened the buckle and was finished. Deke watched from the fence, amazed.

"There!" she said, turning to Deke. She couldn't help feeling proud of herself. "How did I do, Mr. Flanders?"

"Great," he said, spitting the straw onto the dirt. "But Maggie never minds the bridle that much. Just wait until you try to saddle her."

# Chapter 6

"Now, never put a blanket on a horse without showing it to her first," Deke said ten minutes later as they went on with the lesson.

He presented the blanket to Black Fury, then spread it across the gelding's glossy back. Deke watched, amused, as Victoria did the same to Maggie. This was turning out to be a lot more fun than he had expected.

He knew that Maggie wasn't finished with Victoria yet. The old mare was the most stubborn horse he had ever seen. She obeyed Deke out of love. But Maggie didn't love very many people. And Deke could tell by the gleam in the horse's eyes that she didn't like the actress at all.

Deke picked up his saddle and presented it to Black Fury. "And you show them the saddle, too," he told Victoria. "Then they know they're about to feel something on their back."

Victoria picked up her saddle. She held it under Maggie's nose for a moment. Then she grunted as she swung the heavy saddle up onto the horse.

Deke saw Maggie lay her ears back. She snorted and shook her head.

*Yep*, he thought, *this is gonna be good*.

"Now you grab the girth like this," he said. "Cinch it good and tight."

She followed his lead. "Like this?" she asked.

"Tighter," he said. "Or else the saddle will slip and you'll fall off."

She pulled the girth tighter. Deke smiled, knowing it would do no good. Maggie was an old pro at a trick called bloating. She would inhale and hold her breath while being cinched. This caused the girth to be too loose when she exhaled. And soon after the rider got into the saddle, the whole thing would slip to the side, dumping the rider into the dirt.

"There, that's as tight as I can get it," Victoria said.

She looked up at him, her face flushed. He couldn't help noticing how pretty she was. Her green eyes sparkled, and she looked like a little girl who was very pleased with herself.

"All right," he said. "Now, I just want to know one thing."

"What's that?"

"Have you ever been on a horse before? Really?"

She blushed and looked away. "Yes," she said, but her eyes didn't meet his.

"Tell me the truth," he said.

"Okay. I'm not lying. I *was* on a horse once . . . for about one and a half seconds."

He thought about this and frowned. "In other words . . . you got on one side and fell off the other," he said.

"That may be true. But for a second, I was on a horse." Her eyes finally met his, and she smiled. Deke found himself thinking how nice it might be to kiss those lips. Then he brought his mind back to the business at hand.

"Okay, here's how you mount a horse," he said.

Deke showed her how to turn the stirrup toward her and how to grab the saddle horn.

He swung himself up onto Black Fury and told her to do the same.

Victoria's green eyes widened with fear as she stood beside the mare.

"I always forget how big horses are," she muttered, "until I'm about to get on one."

"Just hop on up there," Deke said. "With those long legs of yours, you shouldn't have any trouble."

She shot him an angry glance. But her anger seemed to give her courage. She grabbed the reins and horn and pulled herself up into the saddle.

"All right. Now what, Mr. Flanders?"

Deke nodded and smiled, pleased with himself. So, getting her angry worked. He'd have to remember that.

Besides, Victoria was beautiful when she was mad. Her eyes turned two shades darker, and her cheeks blushed bright red.

Yes, it certainly was worth getting her dander up.

"Now, you just give her a nudge in the ribs with your heels, like this," he said, "and off you go."

He rode Black Fury around the corral, and she followed on Maggie.

"To turn the horse to the left, you just lay the rein against the right side of her neck, like this," he said, showing her with his horse.

"On the *right* if you want her to go *left?* That doesn't make any sense. Are you sure?" she asked.

The tone of her voice annoyed him. She really was a know-it-all.

"It makes sense to the horse," he shot back. "But some people don't *have* horse sense."

She laid the rein on the right side of Maggie's neck. Deke grinned. This was when it usually happened.

He rode up beside her, just in case.

Sure enough, Maggie went one way. And Victoria, the saddle, and blanket went the other.

She screamed, but he was there to catch her by the arm as she fell. Gently, he let her slide to the ground.

Maggie pranced away, her tail high in the air.

"What . . . what happened?" Victoria said from her seat in the dirt.

Deke tried to swallow the laughter that bubbled up inside him.

"I don't know," he said between chuckles. "I reckon you just didn't get it tight enough."

"Then I reckon," she said, imitating his drawl, "that you aren't much of a teacher."

Deke took off his hat and bowed to her. "And you, Miss Thornton," he said, "are no Annie Oakley."

# Chapter 7

Victoria stood at her bedroom window, enjoying the view. Snow still covered the mountain peaks in the distance. But closer to the house, grass was sprouting up in green tufts here and there. On a nearby hill, cattle nibbled at the bales of hay that had been dropped for them. A calf trotted after its mother, bawling at the top of its lungs.

Victoria breathed in the fresh, clean air, so different from Los Angeles smog. Yes, spring had arrived in the Rockies.

Some other time, she might have enjoyed a weekend like this. After all, she was in the mountains of Colorado, one of the most beautiful places in the world. And Deke Flanders was one of the sexiest men she had ever met.

*Too bad he's such a pain in the rear,* she thought.

Anyone with shining black hair, and eyes as blue as the Colorado sky, should be easier to get along with. And the way he filled out his jeans and western shirt set her heart to pounding.

She was used to being around men who worked out in health clubs. But Deke's muscles had developed from hard work, not by lifting weights. Victoria decided she liked the difference.

The night before, they had shared a simple dinner of steak and potatoes.

Usually she didn't eat meat, but she didn't want to insult him by refusing. It was better than she had expected. Deke was a good cook.

Their conversation had been light, almost pleasant. But he hadn't been able to resist teasing her about falling off Maggie. She had gotten angry and stormed off to her room.

Now, looking back, she wondered if she had acted childish. After all, it must have looked pretty funny—a grown woman sliding sideways off a horse in slow motion.

*Well,* she thought with a sigh, *better get on with it.*

Pulling her boots onto her sore feet, she groaned. Every part of her body ached. Darn Martin for getting her into this!

So she wasn't Annie Oakley. She could live with that.

But she was going to ride that horse today, if she had to glue herself to the saddle. She would show that smart-mouthed cowboy a thing or two.

No man got the last laugh on Victoria Thornton. Not even a cute cowboy with bright blue eyes and great buns!

Victoria was rather proud of herself. She had stayed on Maggie for almost half an hour now. Before saddling her, Victoria had given the horse three carrots, instead of one. Maybe that was the trick—bribery. She'd have to remember that.

"So, how does it feel to sit in a saddle—for longer than thirty seconds, that is?" Deke asked. He grinned at her, his blue eyes sparkling with mischief.

"To be honest," she replied, "my bottom is sore. My tailbone feels like it's taken root to the saddle. Other than that, I'm just ducky. Thanks for asking."

He glanced down at her shapely rear end for a second, then back to her face.

The light in his eyes warmed her and kindled a blaze that spread through her body. Why did he have to be so handsome? And why did he have to be a stubborn, Rocky Mountain cowboy?

They came to a fork in the trail. A meadow and bubbling creek lay to the right. A forest of pine trees loomed to the left.

She laid the rein against the left side of Maggie's neck, signaling her to go toward the meadow. But the horse snorted and turned left.

"Hey, what's going on here?" Victoria shouted as the horse broke into a brisk trot. "Slow down! What do you think you're doing?"

"Oh, no," Deke said, shaking his head. "Darned horse. I was afraid she'd do that."

"Do what?" Victoria called over her shoulder. She pulled back on the reins. "Whoa! Whoa, horse. Stop!"

But Maggie ignored her rider. She broke into a gallop and aimed for the nearest pine tree with low limbs.

Deke took off after them. He grabbed his rope and began to circle it over his head.

"Deke!" Victoria screamed. "De-e-k-e! Make her stop!"

Too late, Victoria realized what Maggie had planned. The limb seemed to be rushing at her, getting bigger by the moment. She ducked, but she knew she would still hit it.

A second before her face made contact with the bristly needles, Victoria heard a *whoosh* in the air over her head. Something circled her waist and yanked hard.

The next thing she knew, she was sitting on the ground, instead of on the horse. And her pride was hurting almost as much as her bottom.

She wasn't surprised to see Deke laughing himself silly. In one hand he held the rope he had used to lasso her. The other hand gripped the saddle horn. He was laughing so hard he was about to fall off.

"I'm glad you're enjoying yourself so much, Mr. Flanders," Victoria said, dragging herself to her feet. Groaning, she rubbed her rear end, which was hurting much more now than before. With an angry grunt, she pulled the rope from around her waist and threw it to the ground.

She watched as Maggie whirled around and trotted past her, tail in the air. The horse was heading back to the barn—and more importantly—her food.

"Bad horse," Victoria called out to her. "Ba-a-ad horse. Somebody should make glue out of you."

"Are you . . ." Deke gasped between guffaws, "are you okay?"

"No, of course I'm not okay!" She dusted the dirt from the seat of her jeans. "You just lassoed me like a heifer and yanked me off a horse. How do you suppose I am?"

He wiped the tears from his eyes with the sleeve of his shirt. "Would you have preferred to hit that limb with your face?" he asked.

"My butt hit the ground—*hard*," she said. "Is that the best a champion stunt rider could do?"

"Sorry," he said with a smirk. "I didn't have a lot of time to plan it out."

"No kidding."

He rode his horse closer to her. Leaning down, he held out his hand. "Want a boost up?" he asked. "Black Fury and I will give you a ride home— since you seem to have misplaced your horse."

Instead of taking his hand, she slapped it away. "No thank you, Mr.

Flanders. I'd rather walk fifty miles than ride behind you on a horse." She thought for a moment, then added, "On hot coals, that is. Barefoot."

He laughed and shrugged. "Well, I can see you feel strongly about it. So I won't argue with you. See you back at the ranch."

She ignored him, refusing to answer.

He glanced up at the sun, which was straight overhead. "It's about noon," he said. "Try to make it back before dinner, okay? I start getting hungry about six."

Victoria fumed as she watched him ride away at a quick gallop. She took a couple of steps and realized that her feet hurt even more than her rear. The new boots were starting to rub her heels.

"Cowboys!" she said, tossing her hair back over her shoulders. "I just decided . . . I hate them even more than flies and horses!"

# Chapter 8

The next morning, Deke walked into the kitchen, ready to make breakfast. But Victoria was already having hers— a bowl of cold cereal.

That didn't surprise him as much as the fact that she was eating it, sitting on the radiator.

He couldn't help feeling a bit guilty. After all, he had been pretty hard on her.

"I'll make you steak and eggs, if you like," he offered.

"No, thank you," she said. She avoided his eyes. Hobbling over to the sink, she rinsed her bowl.

*Her feet must be killing her*, he thought as he watched her limp. He should have insisted that she ride back with him yesterday.

After all, Martin had asked him to teach her how to ride a horse—not cripple her.

"You really are doing well," he said. He walked over to her and placed his hand on her shoulder. To his surprise, she didn't pull away. "You're a quick study."

"Yeah, sure." She looked like she was about to cry. "It's the last day, and I can't even stay on a horse. I'd say I flunked riding school. Completely."

He turned her around to face him and put his hands on her shoulders.

"No, that isn't true. It isn't your fault at all. It's Maggie. She's a very difficult horse."

Suddenly, Deke realized that he was standing, face to face, with Victoria Thornton. Her green eyes looked up into his, tears shining on her long lashes. She looked like a sad little girl who had just gotten a bad report card. He had to admit, she really wasn't bratty or conceited like he'd thought.

It was all he could do not to lean down and kiss her. He wanted to kiss her hurt away and make everything better.

He leaned closer to her. For a moment, he thought he saw desire in her eyes, too. But he decided he must be mistaken. He was a beat-up cowboy. She was a world-famous star. Who did he think he was kidding?

"I . . . I just feel like I've let everybody down . . . Martin, myself . . . even you," she said.

"Please don't feel that way. I'm telling you, it's Maggie. She pulls those tricks on everybody. When you try to saddle her, she sucks in her breath. Then, once you're on, she exhales and dumps you."

"Oh, really?" Victoria raised one perfectly shaped eyebrow.

"Yeah. And Maggie loves to go under a low-hanging limb and sweep her rider off."

"I see," she said slowly. "She does this all the time, huh?"

"All the time."

"Thank you for telling me," she said. "I feel *so* much better now."

Deke wondered at the strange look on her face. Her mouth was smiling, but her eyes weren't. They bored into his, until he looked away.

"Well, do you want to go out again?" he asked, releasing her shoulders.

"Not right now. I'm still pretty stiff and sore," she replied, placing her bowl in the dishwasher. "How about later this afternoon?"

"Whatever you say. Make it easy on yourself."

"I'll do that," she said. Again she gave him a smile that didn't reach her eyes. "See you later."

She turned and walked down the hall toward her bedroom. Deke had an uneasy feeling. She had acted like everything was fine. But, somehow, he knew it wasn't.

Something was wrong. He just didn't know what. And that made Deke Flanders very nervous.

# Chapter 9

*So, he knew all along,* Victoria thought as she led Black Fury out of the stable and placed the saddle on his back. Deke had let her think it was her fault that the saddle had slipped. He had known Maggie would run her under a tree. But he had let her ride the old mare anyway.

She was going to get even with him for that. Oh, yes.

She pulled herself up into the saddle. This time her anger kept her from being nervous. She nudged Black Fury forward with her heels. To her relief, he obeyed her perfectly.

As they trotted down the road toward the pine tree forest, Victoria smiled to herself.

Ah, revenge was sweet. And she could hardly wait to taste it.

Deke found the note taped to the kitchen cupboard. It said:

Dear Deke,

I'm so ashamed of my horrible riding that I decided to go out alone. I hope you don't mind. I didn't want you to have to bother with me anymore.

Thanks for everything,

Victoria

*Bother with her?* he thought. *Why did she think she was a bother?*

Deke's conscience gave him a pang. He really had treated her like she was a fly in his ice cream. Maybe she hadn't been the easiest person to deal with. But he hadn't been a knight in shining armor, either.

He thought of how clumsy she was in the saddle. She wasn't ready to go riding alone. If anything happened to her . . .

He wouldn't let himself think about it. But he had to find her. And when he did, he'd give her a piece of his mind. It was one thing to be brave; it was another to be foolish!

# Chapter 10

Victoria rode through the woods until she found the place. The *perfect* place. She reached inside her jacket and pulled out a small plastic bag. It was filled with a liquid she had mixed in Deke's kitchen earlier.

A smile lit her pretty face and she laughed. She climbed down from the horse. Patting his neck, she said, "I'm sure you can find your way home without me, Black Fury."

She opened the plastic bag. "I hate to do this to you, old buddy, but we're in this together."

Carefully she applied some of the sticky red liquid to the saddle and the horse's neck. Then she gave him a pat on the rear.

"Run along home," she called. "And when you get there, try to look worried."

She found a comfortable place to lie down. "Now," she said, stretching out on the soft ground. She placed her arms and legs one way, then another. Twisting her arm behind her head, she said, "I wonder . . . which position looks the most dead?"

Deke rode Maggie fast and hard through the forest. He had been searching for almost an hour. No sign of Victoria. Nothing.

He couldn't stop thinking about the blood on Black Fury's neck and saddle. At first he had thought the horse was hurt. Then he realized the animal wasn't bleeding. That meant only one thing. *Victoria* had been bleeding.

God only knew how badly she was hurt.

He had to find her.

He rounded a corner and saw something lying beside the path. It was her!

She was lying on her side, her arm twisted at a horrible angle. And worst of all, she wasn't moving.

"Victoria!" he shouted as he jumped off the horse and ran to her. He dropped to his knees beside her still form. "It's me, Deke. Are you all right? Say something."

He shook her shoulder gently. She didn't respond.

Carefully, he checked for broken limbs. But everything seemed okay. There were no cuts or bumps on her head, in spite of all the blood in her hair.

The red, sticky stuff was all over the front of her white blouse. But he couldn't find the terrible wound that had caused so much bleeding.

He had to get her back to the house, and to a doctor as soon as possible.

Cradling her in his arms, Deke climbed back on the horse.

"Easy does it, Maggie," he said. "We have to give her a smooth ride back."

For once the horse seemed to understand, and she behaved.

Deke held Victoria tightly against his chest. "Victoria," he whispered. "Please speak to me. Tell me you're going to be all right."

She said nothing, but he could feel her warm breath on his cheek. That was a good sign.

"I shouldn't have made fun of you," he said. "That was a rotten thing to do. You weren't all that bad a rider. You were just scared, that's all. And now . . ."

He placed a quick, soft kiss on her forehead. "I'm so sorry this happened. I wanted . . . to tell you something. I wanted . . ."

He couldn't bring himself to say the words, even if she couldn't hear him.

"Tell me," she mumbled, her eyes still closed. "Tell me what?"

Relief flooded over him. He took a deep breath and said the words that were in his heart. "I wanted to tell you that you aren't a spoiled brat at all. You're really a pretty gutsy lady. You faced one of your greatest fears. Most people never do that. I admire you."

She sighed and snuggled closer into his arms.

"And—" he said, "and I like you. A lot. You have to pull through this.

I couldn't stand it if anything happened to you because of me."

He held the reins with one hand. With the other he brushed her hair back from her blood-stained face. "We have to get you to a doctor," he said. "You're bleeding really badly. And I can't find where it's coming from. Where does it hurt?"

For a moment she said nothing, then mumbled, "Hurt? Umm . . . mm . . . all over." She moaned and rolled her head from side to side. "I didn't think . . . you . . . cared," she said. Her words were weak, barely a whisper. "You said . . . "

He bent his head low to hear her. "I said what?"

"You said . . . you had . . . never seen . . . " She fought for breath. "Never seen so much . . . sky . . . between a woman's . . . rear end . . . and a saddle."

He felt his face grow hot. "I'm sorry, Victoria. That was a lousy thing to say. I'm so sorry."

Her eyelids fluttered open and she looked up at him. "Then . . . I'm a good rider?"

"Except for falling off the horse, you're great!"

She smiled faintly. "Good. How long do you think it will take me to learn?"

His arms closed around her more tightly. He pressed another kiss to her cheek. Then another to her upturned lips. The kiss was long, soft, and warm, and it stole his breath away.

"Well . . ." he said. He could see the lights of the ranch in the distance. "I really want to get to know you better. I want the chance to convince you that cowboys aren't all bad."

She grinned up at him, then kissed him again. "And how long do think that will take?"

"I want to take my time and do a really good job."

"Yes, that's very important," she agreed, nuzzling his neck. "I want you to take all the time you need."

"Horseback riding isn't easy," Deke went on. "And neither is learning how to love a cowboy."

He looked puzzled and licked his lower lip. Some of her "blood" had gotten on his mouth when they kissed. "Tastes like maple," he said, confused. "Maple syrup."

"Gee, imagine that!" She laughed. "Maybe maple syrup with red food coloring?"

He looked down at her, at the wicked grin on her pretty face. His relief was stronger than his anger. "You mean, you faked it?" he said. "The whole thing? You're not even hurt?"

"It's called 'acting,' not 'faking.'" She wrapped her arms around his waist and held him close. "I think *I* can learn to love a cowboy," she said. "The question is: Can *you* learn to love an actress?"

"I don't know," he said. "Are you intending to do any more 'acting' for me?"

"If you deserve it."

He laughed. "Well, that's going to take some getting used to. You'd have to stick around for quite a while."

"How long?"

He leaned down and licked a drop of the syrup off her forehead. "A long time. A *long, long* time."